THE PLUTO— NIUM PIRATE

MOFFAT ACADEMY

First published in 2000 by Franklin Watts
A division of the Watts Publishing Group Limited
96 Leonard Street, London EC2A 4XD

Editor in Chief: John C. Miles
Designer: Jason Anscomb
Consultant: Robin Kerrod

A CIP catalogue record for this book
is available from the British Library.

ISBN   0 7496 3471 5 (hbk)
           0 7496 3475 8 (pbk)

Printed in Great Britain

THE PLUTO-NIUM PIRATE

BY
MICHAEL
JOHNSTONE

ILLUSTRATIONS
BY ANDY DIXON

W
FRANKLIN WATTS
NEW YORK•LONDON•SYDNEY

Bandits stealing plutonium to make nuclear weapons?
People living on the Moon?
Planes that fly there as a matter of routine?
We must be joking, musn't we?
No we're not!

Only a few months ago, when a shipment of plutonium was being transported across the ocean, security forces were alerted that pirates may try to hijack it.
For years now, scientists have been researching the technology that will be required when men and women go and live on the Moon. Life-support systems, artificial gravity, lunar transport; these and more have long since moved from the drawing board and are now practical propositions.
A plane that flies to and from the Moon over and over again is just a few steps on from the first Space Shuttle, which was launched in 1981 and has been used time after time. Already more than one billion dollars have been spent developing its two successors – the X-33 and VentureStar. Vehicles such as these will make a trip to the Moon as everyday an event as catching the school bus.
And if that's what is already on the drawing board, who's to say what scientists will come up with tomorrow?
So come with us on a voyage of adventure set near the end of the twenty-first century, then find out a little about the technology of tomorrow's world. Technology that is being developed today.

THE PLUTONIUM PIRATE

A few moments after the screens and lights at the Fast Breeder Nuclear Reactor Base at Bayburt in northern Turkey had started to flicker, they went out, plunging the place into darkness.

Seconds later the emergency generator came on automatically.

Security Officer Kemal Deres turned to his Number Two and groaned. 'You know what that means, don't you? Every nook and cranny of the base has to be searched.'

'Oh come on, Kem,' sighed Ozan Togul. 'They were only out for five seconds. Ten at the most. Look,' he pointed at the bank of screens in front of him, each one showing a different part of the base. 'Everything is exactly the same now as it was a minute ago.'

'I can see that.' Kemal rose from his seat as he spoke. 'But orders are orders. Any blackout, no matter how short, and we have to do the rounds.'

'You're such a stickler for orders.' Ozan shook his head and reached for his heavy outdoor coat hanging from a hook on the back of the door.

'That's why I'm senior to you,' grinned Kemal.

'Come on. Quicker it's done, quicker we'll be back here in the warm.'

The strong, cold wind whipped up the snow, filling in the trail of footprints behind Kemal and Ozan almost as soon as they had made them.

It never took the two men long to do their rounds. Bayburt was a comparatively small reactor base. It was manned by only a few scientists, some administrative staff, Kemal and the other security guards, and a handful of skilled workers. Any heavy work that was necessary was done by robots.

'Told you it was a waste of time,' shivered Ozan about half an hour after they had started out. As he spoke he pulled up his collar. 'Come on, let's get back.'

'We've still got the Transport Office and the Computer Centre to check,' said Kemal.

'Tell you what.' Ozan banged his gloved hands together. 'Let's do one each.'

'Against the rules,' said Kemal. 'After a power cut, everything must be inspected by two guards.'

'Can't you forget the rule book just this once?'

'Oh very well,' said Kemal, who hated the cold as much as Ozan. 'Toss you for it.'

He took a coin out of his pocket and flicked it in the air.

'Heads!' said Ozan.

'Heads it is,' mumbled Kemal.

'I'll take Transport,' smiled Ozan. 'It's on the way back to Security. See you there in ten minutes.'

'Put a brew on when you get there.' Kemal's breath hung in the freezing air. 'And if you want to put a drop of something stronger in it, I won't complain.'

'Right you are.' Ozan turned and headed for the square building a few hundred metres away clearly outlined against the starry night sky. 'See you.'

'Yes! See you,' sighed Kemal.

The snow crunched under his feet as he set off for the Computer Centre at the other side of the Base. When he got there, he quickly unlocked the door and made his way along the corridor beyond, looking into each office in turn.

'Still working, Miss Aturk?' he said to the attractive dark-haired young woman hunched over a keyboard in the last office he entered.

'Uh-huh,' she grunted, not taking her eyes off the screen. 'Checking the plutonium/uranium balance in Number Two Reactor.'

She might as well have said she was working on a recipe for lamb kebabs for all Kemal cared. He could have written everything he knew about the nuclear reaction process on his thumbnail and still have room to write his name and address. Security was his job, had been ever since he had left school and would be until the day he retired.

'And you?' Anna Aturk asked, her eyes fixed on the screen. 'Still hard at it?'

'Checking everything's OK,' Kemal replied. 'Standard procedure after a power failure.'

'Power failure?' Anna looked around, a puzzled expression on her face.

'About thirty-five minutes ago,' said Kemal.

'Oh, when the lights went out and the screen went blank.' Anna smiled vaguely. 'Is that what it was?'

As she spoke the smile faded from her face. 'Shouldn't there be two of you doing the security check?'

'There is,' Kemal lied. 'My deputy is checking the offices off the other corridor.'

'Fine,' Anna said, turning back to her screen. 'You'll excuse me if I carry on with what I was doing?'

'Of course,' Kemal felt relieved. 'We'll leave you to it. Goodnight.'

''Night!'

Kemal closed the door behind him and set off through the snow for Security, looking forward to a cup of strong sweet coffee laced with fiery liquor.

'Can't smell the coffee,' he called as soon as he was through the door.

It was only after he had shrugged his coat off and hung it on its hook that he saw Ozan's coat wasn't there.

'Ozan!' he said. 'Where are you?'

There was no reply.

'Ozan!'

Looking around, he found himself facing the bank of security screens.

There was Anna Aturk still hard at work.

Suddenly something on the screen alongside caught his eye.

It was the Transport Room.

And there, lying on the floor, obviously unconscious, lay Ozan Togul.

CHAPTER 2

'OK.' Josef Chalka, Director of the Base, glared at Kemal. 'Tell me once again what happened.'

'There was a power failure,' Kemal began for what seemed like the tenth time. 'When the emergency generator came on, Ozan Togul and I started the regulation security check. We covered the Base section by section – '

'Both of you?'

'Both of us,' Kemal nodded. 'Until we had only the Computer Centre and Transport to cover. It was freezing cold. We were keen to get back, so we decided to separate. I went to check CC and Ozan headed for Transport.'

'Miss Aturk has told us you said to her that Togul was with you.'

'I was – was not telling the truth,' Kemal bowed his head. 'I'm sorry!'

'Sorry!' The word shot from Chalka's mouth. 'Sorry! It's only thanks to me that you weren't fired on the spot. Now get out of my sight.'

'Before I go, can I ask what you will be saying?'

'Precisely what we know happened.' Chalka took his glasses off and started to gently massage his brow with his free hand. 'That three anti-nuclear protesters cut through the main electricity supply cable. And that before the emergency generator came on, they climbed over the electric wire and got into the base.'

'Do we know which protest group they're with?' asked Kemal.

'Not yet,' said Chalka. 'All we know is that they were looking for the reactor, but ended up in the Transport Room by mistake. When Ozan disturbed them, they knocked him out, then panicked. They made it to the main garage, boarded a truck and were captured when they tried to break through the east gate in it.'

'And me?' Kemal gulped. 'What about me?'

'I will recommend that because of your length of service and your spotless record, you be severely reprimanded, but be allowed to keep your job. You will never be considered for promotion, of course.'

Kemal nodded. 'At least I still have my job! Thank you.'

'What else could I do, Father-in-law?' Chalka glared at Kemal. 'Your daughter would never speak to me again if I had you fired. Now go. Just go.'

* * * * *

'I wonder how many nuclear warheads they could make out of the Plutonium 239 in that truck?' Kemal and Ozan watched the small convoy pass under the raised barrier and head along the dusty road beyond.

It was the first time Kemal and Ozan had been on duty together in the three weeks that had passed since the break-in.

'Search me!' said Ozan. 'I'm just glad I'm not on escort duty. The road between here and Trabzon is one of the worst in Turkey.'

Kemal nodded. 'I've only been on it once. It gets really scary when it gets to the Anadolus.'

Both men stared at the line of snow-capped mountains that fringed the horizon.

'Still,' Kemal went on, 'I wouldn't mind escorting the freight from Trabzon to Istanbul. I love being on boats.'

'And who would say no to a night or two in the city?' laughed Ozan. 'Come on, best be getting on.'

* * * * *

Late winter had given way to early spring. The sun was shining brightly as the truck, one security car in front and one behind, and two powerful motorbikes on each side, trundled north.

The closer they got to the mountains the steeper the road became, and it wasn't long before the truck's engine was roaring in protest as the driver steered it higher and higher into the foothills.

'What the hell!' he exclaimed just after they had rounded a sharp bend in the road and the car in

front came to a juddering halt, throwing up a curtain of dust that shrouded the driver's cab for a moment.

He brought his foot down hard on the brake pedal, bringing the truck to a slithering stop. But before he could wind down the window to see what was happening, the door was wrenched open.

'Out!' The face of whoever had shouted was swathed in rough woollen cloth, with just the narrowest of gaps left for the eyes. 'And be quick about it, if you want to live.'

Anwar Basra, the driver, stepped down from the truck and was jostled at gunpoint to the side of the road.

'OK, OK, OK!' he said to the bandit behind him. 'There's no need to prod me with that thing. I'm not going anywhere.'

He was pushed roughly to where the security men who had been escorting his truck were standing, the guns of half a dozen or so armed men trained on them. The bandits' long robes drifted open in the breeze, revealing the ankle-length baggy white trousers and dusty black leather shoes that looked curiously out of place worn under traditional Arab clothes.

'What happened?' Anwar asked the guard who had been driving the front escort car.

'When I turned that bend, there was someone lying on the road. Looked like an old lady. I braked and the moment I did – '

'Didn't they teach you anything at training school?' Anwar interrupted him. 'That's a classic ambush tactic.'

'I know. I know!' sighed the guard. 'We're taught that if we see someone on the road, we drive round them and accelerate away. That's the theory. It's different in practice. What would you have done?

Driven over her?'

'Shut up!' one of the bandits shouted. And take your shoes off.'

'What?'

'You heard,' snarled the guard. 'Shoes! Off!'

With six or more guns trained on them, the men from the Bayburt base knew better than to argue. As they knelt down to unlace their boots and shoes, one of the bandits walked among them carrying an old canvas sack.

'In the bag!' he growled. 'Your radios too!' And one by one the Bayburt men dropped their shoes and radios into the sack.

As a second bandit frisked the shoeless men, searching for a hidden radio or mobile phone, Anwar was relieved to see that he wasn't the only one whose big toe was sticking through a large hole in his sock.

Suddenly, he heard a sound that sent a shiver of

fear running down his spine.

The metallic click of an old-fashioned rifle being cocked.

Oh no! he thought, a bead of sweat running down his brow. *They're going to kill us.*

'No!' he screamed, throwing himself to the ground. 'Don't shoot.'

His scream had an electrifying effect on the others. As one they dropped to the ground, lying flat on their stomachs, their faces pressed so hard into the dust and pebbles it hurt.

No sooner had the last of them fallen, than a volley of shots rang out.

Paralysed by terror, Anwar lay there expecting to feel a bullet slam into him at any second.

When none came, relief swept through him.

A second volley.

The same feeling of terror.

The same surge of relief when no bullet hit him.

Anwar forced himself to lift his head to see if any of the others had been hit, and when he saw them lying quite motionless he thought for a horrible moment they were all dead.

'Get up!' he heard a mocking voice call. 'Call yourselves men! Chickens more like it.'

The men staggered to their feet.

'What were they shoot – ?' Anwar began but didn't finish his question. One look at the cars and motorbikes ahead told him the answer. With only one exception, the tyres of every vehicle had been ripped to shreds by the gunshot. Only his truck was undamaged.

'Come on!' One of the bandits waved his rifle in the air. 'Back to camp.' And whooping with delight, the bandits clambered aboard Anwar's truck.

The engine wheezed and clanked for a moment before it roared into life, and a few seconds later it was speeding down the road throwing up great clouds of yellow dust.

Anwar and the others watched until it vanished round the next bend in the road.

'Now what?' someone said.

'Raise Bayburt and get them to send someone to pick us up?' Anwar suggested.

'With what?' someone else said. 'They took our radios, remember?'

'Didn't see you drop yours into the bag, Anwar.' The hope in the speaker's voice was soon dashed when Anwar said that he had left his radio in the truck.

'There's only one thing for it,' he sighed. 'We'll have to walk.'

'We've no shoes,' someone moaned. 'And Bayburt is far away. Our feet will be cut to shreds on that road.'

'Anyone got any better ideas?' said Anwar, and

when no one answered he shrugged his shoulders and said, 'Sooner we leave, sooner we'll be there. Let's get going.'

* * * * *

By the time Anwar and the others limped into Bayburt, the bandits had long been back at their tented camp and were sitting round their fire, celebrating their success.

Had onlookers from the United States of the Two Americas or the Chinese Empire stumbled on the scene they would have been forgiven for thinking they had stepped back in time.

It was 2099.

Men and women lived on the Moon.

The first steps in establishing permanent colonies on Mars were well underway.

But here was a group of men, women and children living as their people had lived for centuries, moving their animals from place to place, scratching a living off the land. It may have looked like a harmless remnant of days gone by. But the people round that fire were no uncivilized innocents.

CHAPTER 4

All of a sudden the flap covering the entrance to the largest of the tents, pitched a short distance from the fire, was pulled aside. There, framed in the space behind, stood a tall, very tall figure dressed in the same style as those round the fire.

But while their robes were dull-coloured and striped, his were white and trimmed with gold. And not for him a band of rough, scratchy material wound round the head. Instead, gleaming, thick dark hair flowed to his shoulders.

'Hassad!' someone murmured and then started to repeat the name over and over again – 'Ha-ssad! Ha-ssad! Ha-ssad!'

Someone else took up the chant. Then another and another, and within moments every bandit round the fire was on his feet and the name 'Hassad!' filled the air.

The white-clad figure stepped from his tent and stood still for a moment, obviously enjoying the tribute of his people. Then he raised his hand to call for silence.

There was an immediate hush.

A little way off, in the corral behind the tents, a horse whinnied then whinnied again. And then there was silence as the men waited for their leader to speak.

'Fellow Dalusians.' Hassad had a rich, deep voice. 'We have done well. Soon I will contact the President of the Two Americas and the Emperor of China to demand that the homeland that is ours by right be returned to us. Dalusia will soon be ours again!'

The cheers that greeted Hassad's words were so loud they startled a flock of birds scratching for insects in the dust a kilometre away.

Then the crowd took up its chant again.

'Ha-ssad! Ha-ssad! Ha-ssad! Ha-ssad!'

The words drifted with the breeze and could be heard far away.

* * * * *

'Same method?' Four-star General Bernard E. 'Betty' Teale looked round the table.

Commander Lorna Maclean looked up from the notes in front of her. 'Exactly the same as the other four raids, sir,' she nodded.

'Why do we bother issuing warnings?' The

general's fist came down hard on the table. 'No one reads them. This makes five times Hassad's got four men into a low-security nuclear base. Five times three of them have been caught in Transport, claiming to be anti-nuclear protesters who got lost looking for the reactor. Five times one of the four hides and finds out when the next shipment of plutonium is due to be trucked out.'

'I wonder how the fourth one got out?' The words were spoken in an educated English accent that was in sharp contrast to General Teale's rough voice.

'I couldn't give a baboon's bum how they got out, Flinty,' the general growled. 'The fact is they did. Let's just thank the Stars and Stripes we infiltrated Hassad's organization and found out what was going on!'

'What do we know about him?' Flinty Tulloch asked.

'Don't you lot ever read briefs, Flinty?' the general sighed. 'I sometimes wonder why we agreed to let Britain join the United States. We should have let you go down the toilet with the rest of Europe.' He scowled at the young Englishman. 'Could someone please tell our British buddy what we know about Faz Hassad? Lorna?'

'Very well, sir,' Lorna cleared her throat. 'Thirty years ago when the European Union started to break up, a lot of small states that hadn't been countries for centuries started to demand independence. They were fed up with being ruled by civil servants hundreds of kilometres away in Brussels.'

'Quite right, too,' mumbled Flinty.

'Shut up, Flinty!' Betty snapped. 'Go on, Lorna.'

'One of the old states that wanted self-rule was Dalusia,' Lorna smiled at the general. 'Ridiculous really. It was tiny, hadn't been independent since it was swallowed up by one of its neighbours in 1287. Then the area was conquered by another neighbour in the fourteenth century. And forty years after that the whole area became Turkish and has been ever since.'

'And when Europe fell apart, up pops Faz Hassad's father demanding independence for Dalusia.' The general was getting impatient. 'He was told where to stick his Declaration of Independence and when his father died Faz starts waving his nasty little flag in our faces. No one took him seriously until now.'

'Why now?' asked Flinty.

'Because', Betty sighed, 'with the amount of plutonium he's got his little mitts on, he could put the state of Virginia into orbit round Venus. That's why.'

CHAPTER 5

'Golly!' gulped Flinty Tulloch. 'That's a bit dodgy, isn't it?'

The general's face went purple. 'There's a wacko out there who could nuke Nebraska and all you can say is "golly" and "a bit dodgy".'

'We know he's got plutonium,' Flinty smiled at the general, quite unabashed at his outburst. 'But do we know if he has the technical know-how to make nuclear bombs? And even if he has, does he have the rockets to deliver them?'

The general held his head in his hands and groaned loudly. 'Of course Hassad's got the savvy to know how to make nuclear bombs! My grandson knows how to make a nuclear bomb – in theory.'

'So what are we going to do?' asked Colonel Juan Aranchez, who was sitting opposite the general.

'Well, we could sit on our backsides and wait for Hassad to contact us. He'll demand we and the Chinese put pressure on the Turks to grant Dalusia independence. And if we don't he'll blitz Broadway or bomb Beijing – '

'Why do you think he won't threaten Turkey directly?' said Flinty, then seeing the expression on the general's face, added, 'Just asking!'

'Most of us have brains between our ears,'

grimaced the general. 'What do you have between yours, Flinty? Of course he's not going to threaten to bomb Turkey. Hassad and the rest of them have family all over the country. They're hardly likely to want to blast their own people off the face of the Earth, are they?'

'I suppose not.' Flinty shook his head.

'Now, as I was saying,' the general went on, 'we could sit around and wait for him to act or we could get in first. We know roughly where he is. We could wipe him out in a minute! Agreed?'

Everyone around the table nodded except Flinty Tulloch. 'Wouldn't it be wiser to wait? To try and reason with him?' he suggested.

'It's thinking like that that lost you Brits an empire,' the general barked. 'We're attacking!'

* * * * *

The USTA nuclear-powered aircraft carrier *Eagle* was on a goodwill visit to the Mediterranean. Her crew had thoroughly enjoyed being entertained in ports all the way along the coast.

Istanbul behind them, they sailed north through the narrow channel that led to the Black Sea, the vast expanse of water that washes Turkey's northern coastline.

The ship was anchored off the port of Trabzon when the order to attack came through.

'Why a helicopter attack?' Taf George, a dark-haired young pilot with a droopy black moustache, asked one of his companions as they headed for the helicopter deck. 'Why not supercruise missiles?'

'We don't have precise bearings for the target,' replied Gray Martin. 'Seems the guy we're after moves his men around the area from place to place. We'll have to rely on visual observation.'

'Know who it is we're gunning for?'

'Some nutcase called Haffad,' said the second pilot. 'No! Hassad. Heard of him?'

The black-eyed man shook his head, but said to himself: *Of course I've heard of him. He's my half-brother.*

CHAPTER 6

The twelve Vampire nuclear attack helicopters spread out and flew low over the land. Everyone on board had their eyes peeled for any signs of Hassad's camp.

'Looks like an endless bowl of lumpy yellow porridge from here,' said Don Contillo, Captain Gray Martin's observer. 'What are we looking for again?'

'A camp. About forty or fifty tents. Horses,' said Gray, who was in command of the expedition.

'How will we know it's Hass-what's-his-name's and not someone else's camp?'

'Apparently one of our agents infiltrated Hassad's organization,' Gray said. 'He told his contact Hassad's tent is bright scarlet and three times larger than all the others. So it should stand out.'

The men flew on in silence, over hilltops and across flat plains, following dried-up river beds and the occasional jagged escarpments that looked like brown squiggles scribbled on a sheet of yellow paper.

'This is like trying to find a pea in the Pacific,' groaned Gray.

Contillo was just about to agree when a tinny voice hissed through the headsets. 'Camp located at 41° 55' north, 46° 20' east. Repeat, 41° 55' north, 46°20' east.'

'Gotcha!' whooped Gray then turned to Don

and said, 'Prepare for action!'

As their stealth-black helicopter headed for Hassad's base they were joined by first one then another and another until by the time they had the camp in their sights, each pilot had brought his aircraft into its position in standard attack formation.

As the lines of 'copters swooped low over the camp, the bandits rushed from the tents. When they saw what was overhead they ran back inside to emerge a second later clutching high-velocity laser rifles.

Within moments flash after flash of deadly laser beams was streaking skyward. But in their panic the bandits fired here, there and everywhere and the experienced pilots had little difficulty in taking avoiding action.

Grinning with glee, Gray Martin took his 'copter down and unleashed a smoke bomb which sent streams of dense blue fumes billowing in all directions.

Gray and Don watched as each pilot in turn swooped earthwards to drop more smoke bombs on the bewildered bandits. 'I'd hate to be trying to find my way out of that,' grinned Don. 'It's like flying over the sea.'

'OK, guys,' Gray said into his voice-mike. 'Let's get down there.'

It was all over in a matter of minutes.

As the spluttering bandits staggered from the smoke clutching their burning throats and wiping their streaming eyes, they were in no state to resist being rounded up. They were herded like sheep into the corral where they were forced at gunpoint to sit on the ground with their hands on their heads.

'OK. Which one of you is Hassad?' Gray Martin said in perfect Dalusian.

'I am he,' said a small bearded man, rising to his feet.

'No, I am Hassad,' said another, standing up.

'Here,' said a third.

Within seconds every bandit was on his feet claiming to be Hassad.

'I think I can tell.' Taf George tapped Gray on the arm.

'I thought you said you'd never heard of him,' Gray frowned.

'I suddenly remembered I had.' Taf shrugged his shoulders. 'I think that's him over there. The tallest one. In the white robes.'

'You,' Gray beckoned the man Taf was pointing at. 'Over here!'

Hassad walked slowly towards the two pilots and stopped just in front of them, a sneer on his face. 'What do you want?'

'Where's the plutonium?'

Hassad spat on the ground just in front of Gray's feet and said nothing.

'I said where's the plutonium?'

Still nothing.

'It's all right, we'll find it.' Gray Martin held Hassad's stare until a voice from behind the bandit leader shouted, 'It's in a cave in the hills about six kilometres from here.'

Hassad spun round, fury scrawled across his face, to see who had spoken. One of the bandits stepped forward. 'You didn't know you had a spy in your midst, did you, Hassad?'

Before anyone could stop him, Hassad roared like a bull and charged towards the informer. 'Treacherous pig!' he yelled just before Taf George sprang forward and brought the butt of his stun gun down hard on Hassad's head. There was a loud grunt as Hassad's legs buckled from under him and he slumped unconscious to the ground.

The bandits surged forward.

'Fire!' yelled Gray Martin, and the outlaws fell back as a warning volley whizzed through the air just above their heads.

'I think I'd better get Hassad back to base as quickly as possible,' said Gray.

'Shouldn't you stay here and organize loading the plutonium?' suggested Taf George. 'I'll take him back.'

'Quite right,' Gray nodded and before he could call two of his men to lift Hassad to Taf's helicopter, Taf pointed at two of the bandits and barked, 'You and you. Over here.'

'Didn't know you spoke Dalusian, Taf,' said Gray.

'It's amazing what you can pick up in an Istanbul bazaar,' grinned Taf, keeping his stun gun trained on the two bandits as they struggled to get Hassad back on his feet. 'See you back at base.'

* * * * *

It didn't take long to locate the plutonium and ferry it from the cave where it was hidden to the waiting helicopters.

'Everyone aboard?' Gray asked an hour or so later.

'Yup,' said Don Contillo. 'We squeezed all the bandits into five 'copters and the plutonium in the other six. Tight fight but we did it.'

'OK. Let's get going.'

A few minutes later, in a swirl of dust, the eleven helicopters soared into the air, heading for the *Eagle*.

* * * * *

As soon as he had landed his machine onto the flight deck and climbed down, Gray made his way to Admiral Lenny Spalding's bridge.

'I'm happy to report the mission was one hundred per cent successful, sir.' Gray saluted the Admiral.

Spalding frowned. 'I hardly call the loss of a thirty-million-dollar nuclear attack helicopter a hundred per cent success, Martin.'

'Sorry, sir.' Gray frowned. 'I don't understand.'

'Twelve 'copters went out. Right?' The Admiral sounded as if he was speaking to a ten-year-old.

Gray nodded.

'And only eleven returned. Or didn't you think anyone would notice? That and the fact Hassad isn't among the bandits you brought back.'

'But he was in Taf George's helicopter.' Gray felt himself go weak at the knees. 'They set off in advance.'

'They may have set off in advance,' said Lenny Spalding. 'They certainly never got here.'

Jefferson Gates III, President of the Two Americas, took off his glasses and rubbed his tired eyes. 'What do you mean Hassad escaped?' he sighed.

Admiral Spalding cleared his throat nervously. 'One of Captain Martin's pilots set off for the *Eagle* with Hassad aboard and never got there. There's no sign of them. Or the helicopter.'

'Helicopters don't just vanish off the face of the Earth,' snapped the President. 'Even if they crash, their tracking devices still emit signals that can be picked up.'

'Not if they've been deliberately de-activated, sir,' said the thin young man standing behind the President.

'When I want you to speak, I'll rattle your cage, Joel,' Gates snapped. 'Go on, Admiral.'

'We've just run a security check on Pilot-Officer Taf George, and – ' The admiral paused, unsure of how to tell the President the check had revealed Taf George was Hassad's half-brother. Not just that: a raid on his apartment had discovered books, letters and papers that showed him to be committed to Dalusian independence.

'What?' The President thumped the table when the Admiral broke the news to him. 'How in the name of George Washington have you only found this out now? Wasn't this Taf guy checked by Security when he enlisted?'

'He was, sir. But not his mother.'

'What's his mother got to do with it?'

'Before she married Taf George's father, she was married to Hassad's father. He divorced her shortly after Hassad was born. She came to this country, married Fred George, gave birth to a son, Taf – '

'Taf!' The President cut him short. 'What sort of a name's that? Welsh?'

'Short for Mustafa, sir.' The Admiral looked down at his highly-polished shoes.

'Mustafa George!' the President snorted. 'Didn't that ring any bells in Security? He shook his head in disbelief. 'Obviously, Naval Security is about as tight as a frayed rubber band. Still, at least we've got the plutonium. Question is – '

Before he could finish the screen facing him began to flash.

'This is all I need,' the President groaned. 'The Hot Line.'

A moment later, the face of Hi-Karu, Emperor of China, appeared on the screen.

'Mr President?' Hi-Karu's lips hardly moved as he spoke.

'Your Imperial Majesty.' The President was unable to stop himself bowing his head slightly. It was something he always did when he met the Emperor or talked to him on the Hot Line, and something that annoyed him intensely.

'I believe you have come into possession of a large stockpile of plutonium.'

The President said nothing.

'I need hardly remind you that reprocessing nuclear fuel is banned by international agreement.'

'Indeed you don't, Your Majesty.'

'Then may I ask what you are going to do with it?' The Emperor's voice was ice-cold.

'Dispose of it.' So was the President's.

'Where?' said the Emperor.

'According to our records there are no nuclear disposal facilities available.' And before the President could get a word in, Hi-Karu went on, 'I need hardly remind you that holding any more than the agreed amount of plutonium was outlawed in the terms of the Treaty of Edinburgh.'

'Of course you don't,' snapped the President. 'I signed it. We both did. Remember?'

'Indeed I do,' said the Emperor. 'A very cold place, Edinburgh.' And again, before the President had time to say anything, the Emperor continued. 'Please get back to me by midnight with details of how you intend to get rid of your illegally held store of plutonium. Midnight, United States East Coast time.'

'And if I don't?'

'Then I shall hold you in violation of the terms of the Edinburgh Treaty and take the appropriate action.'

'Meaning?'

'I shall begin plutonium production again.'

'But we agreed to outlaw unauthorized plutonium production.' Judging from the edge in the President's voice he was struggling to keep his temper. 'We agreed that our two countries should hold equal amounts of the stuff. That the countries of the former European Union should each be allowed to have a strictly limited supply. If you resume production, that is a deliberate violation of the treaty. It's like a challenge. A declaration of war almost.'

'Exactly,' Hi-Karu said. 'I repeat. Midnight tonight.' And with that the screen went dead.

CHAPTER 8

The President stared at the blank screen for a moment. 'How long have we got, Joel?'

Although there was a large clock facing him, the young presidential aide glanced at his watch. 'It's just after ten am, sir,' he said. 'That gives us fourteen hours.'

Gates sighed. 'Fourteen hours to find somewhere to store Heaven knows how many tonnes of plutonium.' He glared at Admiral Spalding. 'I assume we have it, don't we? You haven't gone and lost it, have you?'

'It's stowed in the *Eagle*'s holds,' murmured the Admiral.

'Good.' The President scowled and poured himself a glass of water from the jug by the Hot Line. 'Let's just hope it stays there.' He sipped some water. 'Fourteen hours! I may as well shoot for the Moo – '

He stopped before he finished the word and brought the glass down heavily on his desk. Water spilled from it onto the neat pile of papers waiting for his signature, but the President didn't notice. 'The Moon!' he exclaimed. 'The very place.'

'The Moon!' Joel Archer and Admiral Spalding said at the same time.

'You can't be serious,' said Joel.

'Why not?' The President rubbed his hands together. 'It's perfect. It doesn't belong to anyone. It's a Site of Universal Scientific Interest. That was decreed in the Treaty of Cape Town.'

'Exactly,' said Joel. 'It's not ours, so we can't just dump the plutonium there.'

'But that's just it,' Gates laughed. 'We don't have any territory on the Moon. No one has. So if we build a storage silo for it and keep it there, no one can say it's ours. Technically it will belong to the international community. No one lives there now. Apart from the weather guys.'

Joel Archer shook his head. 'The Chinese will never buy it.'

'They will I if can persuade the leaders of every country in the world to agree.'

'Fourteen hours to convince over one hundred and fifty men and women to give their consent to your plan. It's impossible.'

'Oh ye of little faith!' There was a smile on Gates's face. 'Half of them will do whatever we tell them to, if they want to keep the aid we dish out to them every year.'

'And the others?' queried the Admiral. 'The ones who usually side with Hi-Karu? What about them?'

'Not a problem!' The President flicked one of the switches on the console on his desk. 'Now let me see,' he said as the screen glowed. 'Let's start with – '

he paused and leaned towards the microphone on the voice-reactor. 'The President of Bhu-Pal.'

A picture of a beautiful black-haired woman appeared on the screen. Immaculately dressed and seated on a high-backed red velvet chair, she looked more like a wealthy heiress than president of one of the poorest countries of the world.

'Now let's see what we have on her.' The President was clearly starting to enjoy himself. He leaned forward and touched the box marked CIA-CON on one of the menus running along the top of the screen. 'There we are,' he leaned back in his chair a few seconds later. 'I'm sure her people would be interested to know how she pocketed half the money the Chinese gave her country to build the Tatyan Dam.'

One by one, Gates scrutinized the CIA's top-secret files on the prime minister of this country and the king of that, the president of one and the queen of another.

One by one he contacted them, and it wasn't long before they had all agreed to his plans to store Hassad's stolen plutonium on the Moon.

'There you are, gentlemen,' he said when the last of them had given her consent. 'I knew they would all come round to my way of thinking.'

'Who'd have thought the Po – ' Spalding began.

'If one word of that leaks out,' the President

interrupted him, 'you'll be swabbing the decks for the rest of your career, Spalding. Understand?'

The Admiral nodded.

'Good. And anyway, all I was doing was applying a little friendly persuasion,' Gates smiled.

'You mean blackmail,' Joel Archer murmured under his breath.

'I heard that, Joel,' laughed the President. 'Such an ugly word, blackmail. Now get me Emperor Fat Belly. I can't wait to see his expression when he finds out what I've arranged for the plutonium.'

Joel activated the Hot Line and a second later Emperor Hi-Karu's face was glaring at the three men in the President's office. 'Ah, there you are, Your Imperial Highness,' purred the President, once again bowing his head slightly. 'Good news. Good news!'

Like the claws of a lobster about to pounce on its prey, the grab of the giant crane hovered over the first crate for a moment. Then as it was lowered closer, it slowly opened before closing in again, the crate firmly in its grasp.

'Hope that operator knows what he's doing,' one of the watching security guards said to his companion. 'Imagine if she dropped it. There would be plutonium all over the place.'

'Nonsense,' scoffed the woman by his side. 'The plutonium's encased in thick concrete. It would take a sledgehammer even to chip it.'

Two weeks had passed since the President had informed Hi-Karu of his plans.

It had taken a week to bring the plutonium from the Mediterranean to the top-secret Willis Air Base.

Another week had passed while the silo where it was to be stored forever was completed. Now it was being loaded into an old X-30 Spacefreighter.

The two guards watched as one by one the plutonium- and-concrete-filled crates were loaded onto the old Spacefreighter.

'Haven't seen an X-30 in ages,' said the woman. 'I thought they'd stopped using them years ago.'

'So did I,' nodded the man. 'Maybe they kept one

or two for dangerous trips like this.'

'There's no danger.' The woman shook her head. 'It's a routine flight to the Moon. Come on, let's get back to the mess.'

'We're meant to wait till the hold door is shut.'

'Who's going to try and stow away on a clapped-out old X-30 with a hold full of radioactive plutonium?' yawned the woman. 'I need some coffee.'

The moment their backs were turned, Aziz Hafez, one of Hassad's most devoted followers, slipped out of the doorway he had been sheltering in. 'Well done, Anna,' he said to himself as he crept towards the Spacefreighter. 'I knew I could rely on my little sister.'

A few seconds later he had made his way through the cargo hold and had hidden himself under one of the beds in the crew room.

He checked that the life-support system of his spacesuit was working properly. That done, he clipped his belt to the bed, pulled a spare mattress around him to cushion himself for take-off and settled down.

He didn't have to wait long. A minute or two later he heard footsteps in the crew station above.

* * * * *

'Haven't flown one of these things for years,' Chuck Borthwick said to his co-pilot. 'Hope I remember how.'

'It's like riding a bicycle,' laughed Carol Hill.

'What bicycle has three scramjets to accelerate us to Mach 26, goodness knows how many litres of liquid oxygen in the back to give it the final push into space and ten times as much slush hydrogen in the main fuel tanks?'

'Shut up and let's get on with it.'

The two crew had over two thousand hours' space-flight experience between them. Together they went through the routine checks before Chuck Borthwick signalled space-traffic control that he was ready for take-off.

'Runway six,' came the instructions. 'Fly due south-south-west until you reach Mach 5. Then turn five degrees west until you're at 38,000 metres ...'

Carol watched Chuck key the flight path into the Spacefreighter's navigation

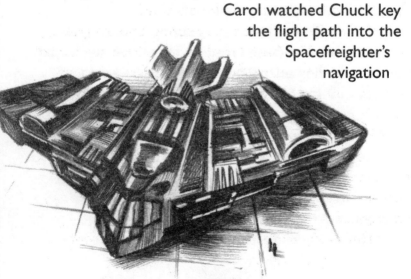

computer. Then they both relaxed in their seats and got ready for take-off.

Suddenly the scramjets roared into life. The Spacefreighter accelerated down the runway at dizzying speed before soaring into the air.

'I've done that more times than most people have had hot dinners,' said Carol as they left the base behind them. 'But it still gives me a kick.'

'I know,' Chuck agreed. 'Nothing to beat it.'

'Well, not much,' smiled Carol. 'Now just relax!'

* * * * *

'How's it going?' Captain Will Rosco stopped by the screen tracing the Spacefreighter's progress.

'Fine, sir,' grinned Helen Tune. 'No problems. They'll be landing in just under an hour.'

'Good!' Rosco nodded. 'Gives me time to grab a cup of coffee.' The fresh-faced young officer headed to the door leading to the mess. He was just about to swipe his ID smart card through lock control when Helen's shout stopped him in his tracks.'

'Sir! We have a problem.'

Every eye in the room was on Will as he ran back to Helen's terminal. 'What's wrong?' He deliberately kept his voice calm as he had been taught to do in an emergency.

'The X-30,' said Helen. 'We've lost radio contact.'

Will leaned over her and his fingers flashed across the keyboard as he tried to establish if there was a fault in the system.

There wasn't.

The camera mounted on the fuselage of the X-30 was still transmitting and Will and Helen could clearly see the surface of the Moon as the spaceship closed in on the landing site in the Sea of Tranquillity.

He picked up a throat mike and slipped it round his neck.

'Flight B908. Come in, please.'

Some static crackled down the line.

'I repeat. Flight B908. Come in, please.'

Silence.

'Flight B908, are you receiving

me? Repeat! Are you receiving me?'

380,000 kilometres away, Chuck Borthwick and Carol Hill heard Will's voice but with Aziz Hafez's gun pressed hard against Carol's back, neither she nor

Chuck dared to respond to Will's call.

'Just do exactly what I tell you to and you won't be hurt.' Hafez had a harsh, rasping voice.

'Which is?'

'Land this old crate at this location.' Aziz pulled a piece of paper from his pocket and held it in front of Chuck's visor. 'The co-ordinates are here.'

'But that's on the far side of the Moon,' Chuck protested.

'Just do as I say if you want to live to see tomorrow.' Aziz pressed the nozzle of his gun so hard into Carol's spine that she winced. 'Do what he says, Chuck,' she whispered. 'Please.'

* * * * *

'What the hell are they doing up there?' Will Roscoe sounded perplexed as he and Helen Tune watched the landing strip disappear as the X-30 accelerated before veering off. 'He's going in the wrong direction.'

'If he carries on in this direction we'll lose the picture when he goes round the far side,' said Helen. 'And we won't get it back for a while. The communication satellite orbiting the Moon is malfunctioning. There's nothing to relay their radio signal from the far side.'

'Come in, Flight B908,' Will shouted into the voice mike, all calmness gone. But as the picture started to fade from the screen, the only answer he got was the continuous crackling of static electricity.

Before Will could say another word, the X-30 disappeared behind the dark side of the Moon and the static faded to nothing.

'Get me Admiral Spalding.'

'Right away, sir.'

Helen keyed in the Admiral's number and a few seconds later said to Will, 'He's on Line Two, sir.'

Will flicked a switch and cleared his throat. 'Sir,' he said quietly, 'there's something I have to tell you.'

* * * * *

'Well done, Aziz!'

'Thank you, Faz.' Aziz Hafez was one of the few men allowed to call Hassad by his first name. The two had been friends since childhood and Hafez was just as zealous in his dream of winning independence for Dalusia as Hassad.

'There were no problems?'

Aziz shook his head. 'Take-off was a bit bumpy,' he said, looking round the small biosphere built many years before to support human life on the lunar surface. 'Why was this place abandoned?'

'When the European Union fell apart the European Space Agency abandoned its lunar research programme and returned all their people to Earth,' explained Hassad. 'But they kept the support systems of this and another small biosphere functioning, in case things should change.'

'How many men do we have here?' Aziz asked.

'Enough!' Hassad shrugged his shoulders. 'The spacebus we hijacked in Cairo was one of the new ones. We were more than comfortable.'

'You were lucky,' laughed Aziz. 'I've just spent the best part of fifteen hours squeezed under a bed in the X-30's crew quarters. The old banger only reached Mach 26.'

'When we were children, 31,000 kilometres an hour was considered fast.' Hassad slapped his old friend on the shoulders. 'What have you done with the crew?'

'They're locked in the hold along with the plutonium,' said Aziz.

'And the plutonium is all there?'

'Every last gramme of it.'

'Good! Once we have completed the next part of our plan, we will be able to send the ultimatum to Gates and Hi-Karu. And if they don't give in, we'll reduce Washington DC and Beijing to radioactive wasteland.'

CHAPTER 11

President Gates held his head in his hands.

'Tell me you're joking,' he groaned. 'Tell me this is a nightmare. Tell me I'm going to wake soon.'

'I'm not joking, sir,' said Joel Archer. 'But it is a nightmare!'

'First of all they lose a load of plutonium, not once but five times. Right?'

'Sir!'

'And then they get it all back. Right?'

'Sir!'

'And now they've lost it again. Right?'

'It's not lost exactly, sir,' said Joel. It's – '

'On the Moon!' The President glared at his personal assistant. 'I know that. You know that. And any time now old Fat Belly's going to know it. And then what's going to happen?'

Joel knew better than to say anything.

'If you think he's going to believe we've lost Heaven knows how much plutonium,' Gates went on, 'then you're not just wet behind the ears, you're raining buckets there. Well, don't just stand there like a stuffed monkey!'

'Perhaps if you told him before he found out from his – er – '

'Spies!' The President groaned again. 'Go on. Say

it. I know. That man's got more spies in the West than there are snowflakes in a blizzard. You're right, I suppose. Better get him for me.'

Joel activated the Hot Line but when the screen started to glow it wasn't the Emperor who appeared. There, staring at them, was Sun-Yet, Hi-Karu's eldest son and heir to the throne.

'Where's Fat – ' the President started to say.

'Bless you!' Joel said quickly.

'His Imperial Majesty?' coughed the President.

'His Excellency has a stomach upset and his doctors have ordered that he is not to be disturbed. I shall ask him to activate the Hot Line as soon as he has recovered. I assume your call has something to do with the plutonium.'

'Indeed it has,' said Gates.

'That it has arrived safely on the Moon, perhaps.'

'Oh yes, it's there all right.' The President had to to stop himself from adding 'somewhere'.

* * * * *

380,000 kilometres away, scientists at the Moon's International Weather Centre were hard at work.

The Centre had been set up twenty years before to study weather patterns on the Earth. Its huge infra-red telescopes detected weather systems as they developed in the Earth's atmosphere. Its computers enabled the Centre's scientists to forecast the world's weather with astonishing accuracy.

For years, few people on Earth had been aware of its existence. To them, a weather forecast was a weather forecast. But that had changed when news about the Centre's latest project to actually control the weather had appeared in the newspapers.

'We plan to fire rockets from our Centre on the Moon into areas of rain-bearing low pressure,' the director had said. 'Recent technological advances have made it possible for us to direct the blast in any direction. This will enable us to move rain-bearing weather systems to wherever they are needed. Droughts and floods will soon be a thing of the past.'

When Faz Hassad had seen the headlines he grinned wickedly. 'Perfect,' he said to Aziz Hafez. And when he had explained his plan to his friend, Aziz had slapped him on the back and said, 'You're a genius, Faz. An absolute genius.'

'It is clever, isn't it?' A smug expression spread across Hassad's face.

The two men had spent the next six months planning how to get their hands on enough plutonium and how to get it to the Moon.

For a time, when Hassad and a few of his bandit gang had been captured in Turkey, it looked like their plans had gone astray. But thanks to Taf George, Faz's agents in Washington and the President's plans to store the plutonium on the Moon, Faz Hassad was now confident he was on the brink of success.

And now the two men were sitting in the cabin of a high-powered lunar rover charging towards the International Weather Centre.

'Just think, Hassad,' Aziz crowed. 'We have the plutonium. We have the means of making nuclear warheads. In a few hours, we will have the rockets. Soon, they will be forced to give Dalusia back to us.'

'For starters,' giggled Hassad. 'With nuclear rockets trained on every major city in the world, we can rule the world if we want to.'

CHAPTER 12

'Ready?' Hassad looked at Aziz.

Aziz nodded.

'Right,' Hassad said. 'Let's get going.'

The two men pulled on their helmets and locked them on to the neckbands of their spacesuits. Then they clambered down from their lunar rover's pressurized cabin and set off for the Weather Centre, just over the ridge they were approaching.

'There it is!' Aziz panted when they had clambered up the rocks.

The two men stopped to get their breath back and gazed at the compound, about a kilometre away.

Even from there, they could see the high fence that surrounded the Centre. Beyond it were banks of radio- and infra-red telescopes surrounding low, flat-roofed biospheres that housed the computers and other data-processing instruments. And in the centre of the compound were the offices and living quarters of the men and women who worked there.

The bandits knew what they were looking at like the back of their hands, thanks to one of Hassad's agents who had bribed a contact in Washington to give him a plan of the Centre.

'Come on,' Hassad motioned Aziz, and ten minutes later they were standing at the compound's entrance.

'Know what to say, Carol?' Hassad whispered into his throat mike.

'Sure do, Chuck,' Aziz answered in a perfect American accent.

'What do you have to do to get in here?' Hassad wondered aloud. He looked up and down as if searching for a bellpush or switch, although he was well aware there was none.

He also knew that he and Aziz had been picked up by security cameras the moment they had made it to the top of the ridge. That was why they had made it look as if they were picking their way painfully towards the Centre.

Hassad started to bang loudly on the door. 'Hey!' he shouted. 'Is there anybody there? You gotta let us in.' His accent was pure New York.

'Stay where you are,' a voice boomed. 'We've got you covered.'

'Best do what they say, Carol,' said Hassad.

A few seconds later the door slid open silently to reveal three tall security guards, their stun guns trained on the two men.

One of the guards beckoned them through the door into a small office.

'Helmets off!'

With three guns aiming at them, Hassad and Aziz weren't going to argue.

'Now who the hell are you?'

'Captain Charles Borthwick! 861562,' said Hassad. As he spoke, he unzipped a pocket and pulled out a plastic United States of the Two Americas' Air Force ID card. Sure enough, underneath his photograph was the name Charles Francis Borthwick. And beneath that the number he had quoted.

The guard snatched the card from Hassad's hand and peered at it before handing in back to him.

'And you?'

'Carol Hill,' replied Aziz. 'Lieutenant, USTAAF. 961071.'

'You're the only Carol I've ever met with a moustache,' snarled the guard.

'I can't help it if my mom and dad had a funny taste in names,' smiled Aziz. 'My dad was a movie buff. He named me after an English director who made a movie he was nuts about. *The Third Man.* '

'Yeah, and my name's Mary,' growled the guard.

'And I thought I had problems!' Aziz shrugged his shoulders and handed him a phoney ID card.

'Shut up!' said the guard, scrutinizing the cracked

card. 'How come it's damaged so badly? And yours,' he turned his gaze on Hassad.

'Must have been damaged when we crash-landed,' said Hassad.

It had been Aziz's idea to crack the cards and dirty them up after they had skilfully replaced Borthwick and Hill's photographs with their own.

'Crash-landed?'

'We were delivering the consignment of plutonium that's to be stored here – '

'Tell us about it,' nodded the guard. 'Who do you think had to organize digging the pit to store it in? What happened to it?'

'You'd have thought that with a cargo like that they'd have given us something better than a banged-up old X-30,' said Hassad. 'We were near the Tsiolkovsky Landing Strip when one of the fuel tanks developed a leak.'

'One of the slush hydrogen tanks?' asked one of the guards.

'You know about X-30s?' said Aziz.

'My uncle was a pilot during the Third World War,' nodded the guard. 'He told me about them.'

'Anyway,' Hassad went on. 'The old crate started to go out of control. And by the time I was able to land it we'd shot round to the far side of the Moon and I had to land her.'

'Where?' the three guards chorused.

'Near the Gagarin Crater,' answered Aziz. 'That's where the plutonium is. Outside an abandoned biosphere.'

'You walked all the way from the Gagarin Crater? That's hundreds of – '

'No, we had a pressurized lunar rover. But it ran out of fuel just the other side of a ridge near here.'

'You guys must be exhausted,' said the senior guard, putting his stun gun back in its holster.

'And hungry,' said Aziz.

'We'll soon fix that,' said the guard. 'We'll get you something to eat and then we can go get the plutonium. We don't want to leave it lying around.'

'It's quite safe where it is,' said Hassad. 'Surely no one's going to try and steal a load of radioactive plutonium.'

'Someone already has,' said the guard. 'Some nutcase called Faz Hass-something-or-other.'

'Hassad?'

'That's it. Apparently he's one of the most dangerous men in the world.'

'One of?' Hassad raised an eyebrow. 'I've heard he's *the* most dangerous man in the world.'

CHAPTER 13

'You guys ready?'

'Ready, Sergeant Chips,' they nodded to the Centre's Senior Security Officer.

Hassad and Aziz followed the burly, balding man along a corridor and into a waiting lift.

'Transport Roo –' Chips was so tall he had to stoop to speak into the voice-reactive control.

Even before the rest of the word was out of his mouth, the lift plunged downward so quickly that Aziz felt the coffee he had just had for breakfast rise in his throat.

A few moments later the lift came to a gentle halt. When the door slid open, Hassad and Aziz saw a line of lunar cargo transporters, their engines already turning over, waiting for them.

'Ten enough?' Chips asked as he led the way to the front transporter.

'Sure,' said Hassad. 'How many men have you brought?'

'Driver and co-driver in each transporter. Most of my security team, in fact.' Chips put one foot on the running board of the leading transporter and pulled himself into the driver's seat. 'Just me in the front one. So that's nineteen. Twenty-one if we count you two.'

'You've got a hoist?'

'Yup,' said Chips. 'One in each transporter.'

'Perfect!' Hassad smiled. 'Absolutely perfect.'

Once Hassad and Aziz had climbed aboard the transporter, Chips activated the engine and the transporter moved slowly towards the air lock between the Transport Room and the Moon outside. Just before they reached it, Chips pulled a smart card from his pocket.

'Come on,' he sighed, swiping it over and over again through a beam of blue light that shone from above the air lock onto a sensor on the moulding above the dash panel.

'Thank you,' he said as the door to the airlock slid open. 'Remind me to get a new card when we get back,' he went on, sticking the card in his pocket. 'This one's on its last legs.'

'Did you say most of your security team was with us?' asked Hassad as the transporter left the air lock and Chips put his foot down on the accelerator.

'Sure,' he nodded. 'There's only a handful of us now that we're the only permanently manned base left on the Moon. And even if we weren't, who's going to attack a Weather Centre?'

* * * * *

It was the morning after Hassad and Aziz had arrived at the camp. After further questioning by the Centre's security men, the two men had been given something to eat. Then they were shown to a spare room in the living quarters.

'You don't mind doubling up?' the guard said when he opened the door. 'We don't get many visitors here.'

'Of course not,' said Hassad, looking around the sparsely furnished room.

'Great,' said the guard. 'I'll leave you to get some shuteye. You guys must be exhausted.'

'Thanks,' yawned Aziz. I'm bushed.'

'I'm just going to write up my report,' said Hassad, taking a notebook and pen from his pockets and sitting on one of the beds.

''Night.' The guard closed the door behind him.

No sooner was the door closed than Aziz opened his mouth to say something. But before he could utter a word Hassad said, still in his false American accent: 'Run after him, Carol. I forgot to ask him where the gym is. And I wouldn't mind a quick workout when I've finished writing this.'

Aziz looked puzzled for a second.

'Go on,' Hassad insisted. 'Before he gets too far.'

Aziz shrugged his shoulders then left the room.

He was back in a few moments but before he could tell Hassad where the gym was, Hassad thrust his notebook at him and said, 'Could you check the times I've put down?'

Aziz took the journal and glanced at what Hassad had written: *This room is bound to be bugged and we're probably being filmed. Don't forget you're Carol Hill, I'm Chuck Borthwick and we're both American.*

'Fine!' said Aziz, handing the book back to Hassad. 'Think I'll turn in. 'Night.'

'G'night!'

* * * * *

The line of transporters wound its way across the dusty, rocky surface of the Moon. Past the jagged rims of huge craters that looked as if they were made out of aluminium foil. Across vast basins created millions of years ago when enormous meteorites crashed onto the Moon's crust. Through a rocky pass between two long-extinct volcanoes that had once spewed streams of molten lava across the lunar land.

In the sky, the Earth glowed misty blue. 'Funny,'

said Chips, turning to Aziz who was in the seat alongside. 'You can look at it a million times and never get used to how beautiful it is.'

'Looks as if someone painted it there,' said Hassad, who was sitting behind.

'Watch out!' cried Aziz.

'Holy Sugar!' gasped Chips, swerving to avoid a huge boulder. 'Didn't see it. I was looking at the Earth. All right in the back?'

'Fine,' said Hassad.

'How much further?'

'Not far.' Aziz tightened his seat belt as he spoke. 'Near the Gagarin Crater. On the far side.'

The transporters trundled across the landscape until they reached a narrow ravine between the rims of two craters. They were halfway along it when suddenly Chips saw something blocking the way ahead . . .

'What the hell?' The words were hardly out of Chips's mouth before he felt a laser rifle prod him between the shoulders.

'Do exactly what I say or you'll be deep-fried, Chips!'

Chips brought the transporter to a halt so quickly that the drivers behind almost didn't stop in time. Each one jammed a foot on the brake pedal and their vehicles skidded to a halt in a cloud of dust.

Even before it settled, the terrorists who had accompanied Hassad and Aziz to the Moon in their hijacked spacecab bounded down the scree on either side of the trackway and surrounded the convoy.

As they did so, the man who had been lying in the middle of the path got to his feet. In two huge leaps he was by the side of the leading transporter. No sooner had he wrenched the door open than Chips found himself lying on the ground, a stun gun pointed at his head.

Glancing to his left, he saw all the other drivers and co-drivers were in the same situation.

He gasped in pain as his arms were pulled roughly together behind him and bound tightly with what felt, through his spacesuit, like nylon straps.

Moments later he was hauled to his feet. 'Ouch!' he grunted as he was pushed towards the back of the convoy where Hassad's men were bundling the other guards into the transporter.

One look at the stun guns the bandits were brandishing and any thoughts he had had of making a

dash for freedom disappeared.

'What's going on?' one of the others asked as the heavy metal door at the back was slowly closed and the transporter was plunged into complete darkness.

'Search me!' grunted Chips, struggling to free his hands. But it was useless.

They felt the transporter bounce slightly as someone clambered into the driver's cab.

Even before the transporter had settled, whoever was at the controls revved the engine.

'I think we're in for a bumpy ride!' Chips shouted as the transporter shot forward, sending the guards sprawling around in the back.

'This is like sitting on top of one of those old pneumatic drill things,' someone shouted.

'I think I'd rather be on a pneumatic drill!' wailed Chips as the transporter hit bump after bump.

It could have been an hour later for all the guards knew when the vehicle came to a sudden halt.

'Aaghh!' cried Chips as everyone in the hold was thrown forward and landed in a heap.

'Ouch!' Jay Dowell, one of Chips's deputies, cried.

'Get off!' groaned Tony Jolley, who had been posted to the Moon only a day or two before. The guards had no sooner disentangled themselves than they heard the door being opened. Moments later, the men were dazzled by a powerful floodlight and then, blinking like bats, they were hauled out.

'I know this place,' said Chips to Jay Dowell as they and the other guards were being shoved towards a small floodlit biosphere about a hundred metres away. 'It's the old Goddard 'sphere. One of the first the old US built on the Dark Side of the Moon.'

'Do you see what's parked alongside?' said Jay.

'I don't believe it!' Chips sounded as if he was smiling. 'It's an X-30. I thought they'd all been grounded years ago.'

The bandits herded the men into the biosphere.

'OK! OK!' Jay protested. 'You don't have to push so hard. I'm not going anywhere.'

'Yes you are,' snarled the bandit behind him. 'You're going in there.'

The guards were pushed into what had obviously been a workshop of some sort.

As the door was locked behind them, they looked around. Through an enormous floor-to-ceiling window they could see Hassad directing operations as the plutonium was hoisted from the X-30's cargo hold onto the back of the transporters.

'What's that?' said Jay, pointing to what looked like two piles of sacking in a corner of the room.

Suddenly one of them moved.

'Who in tarnation are you?' he cried as a bleary-eyed unshaven face emerged from under the sacks.

'Captain Charles Borthwick. USTAAF,' came the reply. '861562.'

'Anyone else under there?' asked Chips.

'Carol Hill,' said Chuck Borthwick. 'Lieutenant. USTAAF. 961071. She's – '

Before he could finish the sentence, Tony Jolley cut him short.

'Look!' he gasped, pointing at the window.

Every eye in the room watched as a crate marked DANGER! RADIOACTIVE PLUTONIUM! dangling from one of the hoists began to swing out of control.

'It's going to hit us,' gulped Jay.

CHAPTER 15

As the crate thudded into a window, everyone in the room ducked, expecting to be caught in a cloud of shattered glass at any second.

But it wasn't the glass that smashed in a shower of splinters. It was the crate. And from it, six heavy slabs of concrete fell to the ground and landed unharmed in the thick dust.

'Don't know why I panicked,' said Chips. 'That glass is three or four metres thick.'

He turned to Chuck Borthwick. 'How come you're here?' he asked. 'You and Carol Hill?'

'We were coming in to land and we were hijacked.'

'You had a passenger?'

'A stowaway!' Chuck grimaced. 'We had to do what he said. We dared not risk a crash. Not with a hold full of radioactive plutonium. Even if it was clad in thick concrete.'

'And then what happened?'

'The moment we landed we were surrounded by these guys. The ones loading the plutonium into these transporters now.'

'Know who they are?' asked Tony Jolley.

'Sure!' nodded Chuck. 'They call themselves the Dalusian Liberation Front. Seems they're trying to win independence for what used to be a tin-pot little state in Eastern Europe, or Turkey somewhere. Can't remember exactly where. Hasn't been independent for centuries.'

The moment Chuck stopped speaking, the sack next to him moved and a few moments later Carol's head appeared from under it.

'Where in the name of Saturn's rings am – ' she yawned, raising herself on one arm. 'Oh, hang on. I remember now.' She shook her head. But when she saw Chips and the other men from the Weather Centre looking down at her she grabbed Chuck. 'Who are these people? Not more gangsters?'

'No, ma'am.' Chips sounded reassuring. 'We work for the International Weather Centre. You were to deliver the plutonium to us to be buried.'

'You mean we've been rescued?' The smile she flashed at Chips lit up her face so radiantly that for a moment he was reluctant to tell her the truth. But after a moment he shook his head and said: 'No, ma'am. We're in the same boat as you.'

Carol's face fell and she looked as if she was about to burst into tears when suddenly the door opened and two of Hassad's henchmen came into the workroom.

'Get your clothes off!' one of them ordered.

'What?'

'You heard,' he nodded. 'Clothes! Off!'

'All of them?' Chips shouted.

'Just your spacesuits!' The terrorist casually waved his stungun around the room. 'Quick!'

Everyone, apart from Chuck and Carol whose suits had already been taken from them, started to clamber out of their spacesuits. A few moments later they were standing in their underwear, more than a little embarrassed.

'Now throw them over here and stand against the window. Face out,' the second terrorist said. 'You two as well.'

Chuck and Carol, who had draped herself in a piece of sacking, joined the others at the window.

They heard the two men gather up the spacesuits before leaving the room and slamming the door shut.

Chuck got to the door first. He tugged hard on the handle. 'Locked!' he cried.

'What did you expect?' Jay Dowell said, looking

round the room.

'Hang on!' cried Tony Jolley, spotting an old-fashioned screwdriver on a workbench. 'Is this any help?'

Chuck grabbed the screwdriver and slid it into the keyhole. Most of the others gathered around him as he wiggled it first one way, then the other. 'Come on,' he muttered. 'Please!'

'Look!' cried Carol, who was staring out of the window. 'The terrorists. They're leaving. They've put on our spacesuits and are getting into the – '

'Yes!' Chuck's whoop drowned the last word of her sentence. 'Done it!'

But as the door swung open, Chips shook his head and said, 'So what? We've no spacesuits. We can't leave the biosphere. The only people who know we're here are hardly likely to tell anyone, are they?'

The gloom spreading round the room was almost visible.

'Let's face it,' Chips went on. 'We're trapped.'

No sooner had Hassad brought the truck to a halt in front of the Weather Centre than a beam of blue light flashed onto the sensor on top of the dash panel. He pulled Chips's smart card from his spacesuit pocket and cut it through the beam.

Nothing!

'Come on!' he said through gritted teeth as he swiped it again and again.

Still nothing!

'Gotta problem?' A voice came through a speaker set in the roof above the driver's seat.

Hassad gazed at the dashboard and saw what looked like a small microphone. 'Yup,' he said, remembering to speak in his false American accent. 'Smart card's got the wobbles.' As he spoke he laid the card alongside the sensor.

'That you, Chips?' said the voice. 'Doesn't sound like you. It's Malcy.'

Hassad coughed and cleared his throat loudly. 'Bit of a throat,' he croaked.

'Lunar larynx, I expect.'

'What'll I do about the card?' Hassad said, huskily.

'Lost the power of your legs as well as your voice?' There was a laugh in Malcy's voice. 'You know exactly what to do. Lazy pig.'

Hassad stared at the door just ahead. Set in the fence to the right of it was a primitive entryphone system.

'Right!' he gulped, looking at the card which was blank apart from a black metal strip that ran across it.

He groaned softly, but not softly enough.

'What's wrong?' said Malcy. 'Forgotten your number?'

'Don't be silly. I know it off by heart.' Hassad was playing for time.

As he made to open the driver's door he accidentally brought his foot down hard on the accelerator pedal. The Prover shot forward, sending the smart card shooting across the sensor.

Something, maybe the suddenness of the movement, made the card work and the door opened.

One by one the trucks went through the airlock into the transporter park beyond.

Looking round, Hassad saw someone waving at him from a seat in front of a bank of screens. He wound down the window and returned the wave before jumping down from the cabin.

As he ambled across to the security area, he started to unlink his helmet, something he knew everyone did at the first opportunity.

'What happened?' Malcy had his back to him. 'What made the card work all of a sudden?' As he spoke he turned round as Hassad tugged his helmet off and dropped it on the floor.

'What the – ' The security guard never finished the sentence. Even as his hand shot for the red alarm switch, the side of Hassad's hand slammed into the side of his neck. He grunted, then slumped unconscious face down onto the console of switches,

buttons and levers in front of him.

Blood oozed from his nose, ran between two dials and dripped onto his thigh.

By now, all the trucks had made it through the

airlock into the parking lot and the men aboard were climbing down from them. 'You,' Hassad pointed to one of his men. 'Find something to tie this idiot to his chair. And gag him. The rest of you, come with me.'

With most of the security force stranded hundreds of kilometres away, there was little opposition. Building by building, floor by floor, Hassad's men took over the Centre and, within the hour, it was his.

* * * * *

'Good evening, Mr President.'

The fact that Hassad's voice was as smooth as syrup did nothing to disguise the menace on his face.

Whatever Gates growled in response, it certainly wasn't friendly.

'Thank you for agreeing to join our discussions, Your Imperial Majesty.' Hassad bowed his head low.

Hi-Karu's lips moved as if to say something. The only sound that came out was a muted spluttering.

'No doubt you are both wondering why I invited you to link up with me tonight.' Now there was a hint of a sneer in Hassad's voice and before either of the two most powerful men in the world could say anything, he went on. 'I'll tell you. I want Dalusia returned to its rightful people.'

'And who would that be?' the Emperor asked.

'The Dalusian Liberation Front,' said Hassad. 'The DLF.'

'So that's what it stands for,' Gates's lips curled a little. 'I thought it was the Dalusian Lunatic Fringe.'

'Oh dear, Mr President,' Hassad sighed. 'That could be a very expensive little joke.'

'Who's joking?' barked Gates. 'I wasn't.'

'And I'm not either.' Hassad sounded as if he was about to lose his temper. 'Unless I hear from you by noon Greenwich Mean Time tomorrow.'

'Greenwich Mean Time?' snorted the President. 'You really do live in the Middle Ages, don't you?'

'Unless I hear from you by then that you agree,' Hassad ignored the interruption, 'I'll nuke Washington and Beijing from here to the middle of Mars.'

'Where's here?' asked Hi-Karu.

'The Moon!'

'The Moon!' The President sounded almost dismissive. 'To do that you need rockets.'

'I have them. The ones scientists here were going to use to move weather systems from one part of the world to another.'

'To make warheads you need plutonium,' said Hi-Karu. 'And that you don't have.'

President Gates cleared his throat and said: 'There's something I've been meaning to talk to you about, Your Imperial Majesty.'

Major Patrick Ravenscroft, known to everyone as 'Raven', was speeding down the Interstate away from Washington when his bleeper went off.

'Tell them I'm on vacation,' he said through gritted teeth.

'Negative, Major Ravenscroft,' the voice-reactive system said in the monotonous metallic tone that grated on Raven's nerves. 'It's the President.'

'Are you there, Raven?' Gates's voice boomed through the speaker set in the steering wheel hub.

'Just off for a week's fishing in Maryland, sir.'

'Then this is the fishes' lucky day,' said the President. 'Turn around and be in my office ASATPS.'

'You mean ASAP, sir?' Raven sounded puzzled. 'As soon as possible?'

'No. ASATPS,' said Gates. 'That's as soon as the President says.'

An hour later Ravenscroft

was sitting in the Oval Office, listening to what the President had to say. 'The Emperor went berserk when we told him about the plutonium. I won't repeat exactly what he said but he implied that if we didn't stop Faz Hassad and his Merry Men, then the Chinese Empire would nuke the bits of the USTA Hassad's missiles miss.'

'Can I get this straight, sir?' Raven put down his coffee cup on the highly polished desk between him and the President.

'Use a coaster can't you?' The President sounded irritable. 'I'd rather face Emperor Fat Belly on the rampage than Mrs Gates if someone marks her precious furniture. Anyone would think she paid for it herself!'

'Sorry, sir.' Raven grinned and put his cup on a flat circle of silver embossed with a golden eagle. 'What you're saying is that this Hassad guy has nuclear warheads trained on Washington and Beijing – '

'That guy's got enough plutonium to nuke New York, Shanghai, Seattle, Macao, Hong Kong, LA, Rio, Buenos Aires. You name a major city in the USTA or the Chinese Empire and that son of a nematode worm could wipe it out at a stroke.'

'Wouldn't it be easier just to give in?' suggested Raven. 'Give them Dal-what's-it?'

'Never give in to terrorists, son,' sighed the

President. 'Look what happened to the European Union in 2046!'

'But Dal-thingy *is* in Europe. Almost.'

'But if we give in, think of the message that'll send to terrorists all over the world. All the little provinces that used to be independent have a few cranks that want them back.' His voice rose. 'If we give in to Hassad, it'll be the end of the Chinese Empire.' He was almost shouting by now. 'And the end of the United States of the Two Americas. The end of civilization as we know it.'

He brought his fist down on the table so hard that Raven's coffee cascaded from its cup. 'Oh no!' the President cried, pulling a silk handkerchief from his breast pocket and mopping up the stains. 'If that stains she'll have my shorts for a showercap!'

'And where do I come in?' Raven asked, trying to stifle a laugh.

'I want you to lead an expedition of crack troops to get the base back.'

A siren wailed somewhere in the distance.

Outside, traffic rumbled past the White House garden.

Inside the Oval Office neither man spoke and the clock on the wall seemed to be ticking twenty times louder than it had been a second before.

'Me?' Raven said eventually. 'Why me?'

'Because you're the best man for the job.'

'Why not just blitz the place?' Raven shook his head. 'Send a fleet of bombers and take it out.'

It was the President's turn to shake his head. 'No way,' he sighed. 'A, there are scientists, admin. staff, security guards and other innocent people in Weather Centre. B, they'd see them coming and it would be Wham, bam, Goodbye Uncle Sam. And C – er, C – that's what I've decided.'

'So what's the plan?'

'You land on the far side, but as close to the Centre as you can, and then you – er – '

'Break into a high-security compound, find out where Hassad's missiles are, and make them safe.'

Gates nodded. 'And bring Hassad and his bandits back to stand trial if you can. Let's call it Mission Plutonium Pirate.' He smiled at Raven. 'Yes. I like that. Plutonium Pirate.'

'I think you'd be better off calling it Mission Impossible!'

CHAPTER 18

'Won't they pick us up on their radar, sir?'

Raven turned to the young spacetrooper beside him and shook his head. 'Not in this machine,' he said. 'This baby has the new X-452P stealth coating. No way we can be seen on radar. Unless we run into some clouds, of course. And there are no clouds in space.'

'Right!'

'We'll be OK as long as no one sees us land. We're touching down a long way away from the Weather Centre, so we should be all right.'

'How long do we have?' one of the other troopers asked.

'Not long enough,' Raven grimaced.

'Landing strip ahead, sir.'

Raven keyed in the landing instructions and sat back watching the Moon's pockmarked surface coming closer and closer. 'Here we go,' he said as the landing strip looked as if it was coming up to meet them.

'I've done this more times than I've cast a fishing line,' said Raven as the spacecraft bounced along the runway coming to a halt, 'but I still hate landing. Come on. Let's get on with it.'

The crew unbuckled their safety harnesses,

opened the hatches and clambered down the steps as quickly as their spacesuits would allow them.

'Get the transporter out and let's get going,' Raven ordered. 'Time's tighter than a DC traffic jam.'

As his men drove the super-powered, heavy duty vehicle out of the hold, he looked yet again at the map of the Moon he'd been given.

'OK, guys,' his voice crackled through twelve headsets. 'The ground's pretty rough between here and the Centre. It gets a bit smoother when we pass a disused biosphere not too far from here, but not much. So fasten your seat belts, it's going to be a bumpy ride. All aboard!'

And with Raven at the wheel, the vehicle set off.

'There's the biosphere you mentioned, sir,' said the trooper in the co-driver's seat, after they had been going for about half an hour. 'Thought you said it was disused.'

'It is!' grunted Raven.

'Then why is it lit up like Fourth of July fireworks?' one of the men behind said.

'According to what I was told it hasn't been used for years.' Raven sounded puzzled. 'Best go and investigate.'

'Can we spare the time?'

'Not really, Robbie,' said Raven. 'But let's go anyway.'

The Prover swerved off the the bumpy track and

headed for the biosphere. At first it looked like a huge, glowing beehive that someone had plonked on the lunar landscape. But as they neared it, the details of the structure could clearly be seen.

'What are those tubes coiled round the bottom?' someone asked.

'They're filled with lunar soil to insulate the thing,' said Raven. 'To keep the heat in.'

'Someone's been here recently, sir.' Robbie was pointing through the windscreen. 'These are fresh treadmarks.'

A sudden movement in one of the windows caught Raven's eye. 'Someone's still here!' he cried.

* * * * *

'Someone's coming! Look!'

The men and one woman in the biosphere ran towards the window where Tony Jolley had been standing gazing out at the empty moonscape.

'That's not one of our transporters,' said Chips. 'That's a Millennium 12KCC. They're only just off the drawing board.'

'Twelve ks!' Carol Hill was obviously impressed. 'That's powerful.'

'Top speed three hundred and fifty – they're strictly military-use only!'

Everyone watched as the Prover came to a stop

and twelve men streamed from it.

'Up here!' Jay Dowell banged on the window.

'Think they're going to hear that?' Chuck shook his head and started to wave the sack that had been draped round his shoulders.

'They've spotted us,' someone shouted, seeing one of the men below tap the man in front's shoulder and point up to the window.

A few minutes later the door flew open and Raven and three of his men, laser guns at the ready, burst into the room. 'Don't move,' he shouted. 'Backs against the window! All of you. And hands up!'

CHAPTER 19

'What's going on?' Raven queried. 'This place is meant to be disused.'

As quickly as he could, Chips told Raven what had happened and when he had finished said, 'Now, can I ask you what you're doing here?'

'We've come to save the Earth,' grinned Raven.

'After what happened today, I'd believe anything,' said Chuck Borthwick.

'What have you got to do?' asked Jay Dowell.

'Get into the biosphere, get to the rocket launch pad and get rid of the nuclear payload,' said Raven.

'The rocket launch pad is about two and a half kilometres away from the Centre,' said Chips.

'We need to have a look at the place first.' Raven shrugged his shoulders. 'Then storm in somehow.'

Chips shook his head. 'And while you're doing that, someone presses the button. Only takes a second and it's goodbye Washington.'

'Got a better idea?'

'Yup,' said Chips. All you've got to do is this ... '

'Brilliant.' Raven clapped Chips on the shoulder when he had finished. 'You'll have to come with us, of course. Robbie, you're his size. Give him your suit.'

'But – '

'Just do it,' Raven snapped. 'And quickly.'

'It looks deserted,' said Raven, peering at the launch pad, then passing the binoculars to Chips.

'You're right,' he said. 'That means they must all be in the biosphere.'

It was an hour later. Chips had taken the wheel of the transporter and brought it to within two hundred metres of the launch pad. He knew the Moon like the back of his hand – every crater they passed, every track they drove along, everything.

'You guys stay here,' Raven had said. 'Chips, you come with me.'

Under cover of the rim of a crater, the two men crept to within fifty metres of the pad.

Chips pointed to two rockets standing upright in the middle of the launch area. 'These must be the nukes. Come on. Let's get back to the others.'

As Chips turned to go, Raven grabbed him by the arm. 'Hang on,' he said, pointing to a small vehicle approaching the launch site. 'Someone coming.'

The spacecar halted and two men jumped down and made their way to one of the buildings.

'Blast!' said Raven.

'Doesn't matter,' said Chips. 'They're not going to do anything until the deadline and that's still some time away. By then they'll be sleeping like babies and the rockets will be harmless. Come on.'

* * * * *

'Are you sure this is going to work?'

'Positive.' Chips sounded confident. 'It's always unmanned.'

Raven's men were approaching a squat little building a hundred metres or so from the biosphere.

'Just run this past me once more,' said Raven.

'It's where they make the oxygen for the entire base.' Chips sounded as if he was speaking to a ten-year-old child. 'It's extracted from ilmenite and other minerals in the soil. Then it's pumped to the various buildings in and around the Centre, including the launch pad.'

'You're sure that if we reduce the oxygen supply, everyone in the Centre will fall asleep?'

Chips nodded. 'Once they're out we can take the base over in minutes. And you'll have plenty of time to get to the launch pad and denuke the rockets.'

'OK,' nodded Raven. 'Let's do it.'

The men crept towards the oxygen plant. When they reached the door, Chips keyed in a number and it slid back silently.

'Wow!' gasped Raven, taking in the gleaming banks of dials and the network of pipes leading to a row of shining titanium-alloy oxygen tanks. A label fixed to each tank told which part of the biosphere it

supplied. Above each label was the small wheel that controlled the flow of oxygen.

The men moved along the line of tanks, reducing the flow of oxygen to each part of the base in turn.

'Sir!' one of the troopers signalled to Raven. 'This one's stuck!'

Raven sighed and pushed the young soldier out of the way. 'I'll do it,' he said. But no matter how hard he strained, the wheel wouldn't budge. 'Oh no,' he gasped when he realized which part of the base that tank supplied. 'It feeds the launchpad area!'

CHAPTER 20

Sweat was pouring down Raven's brow as he strained to turn the wheel.

'Yes!' he croaked when suddenly the wheel gave a little. 'Come on!'

As it turned, the needle on the dial measuring the oxygen in the air supply to the launch site began to drop. 'That should have them dozing nicely,' he said after a moment or two. Then he turned to his men and told them to get into the biosphere and tie up the terrorists. 'Chips, you come with me to the launch pad.'

'Don't you need more men, sir?' someone said.

'No!' Raven shook his head. 'There's only two of them there and they'll be out cold till we denuke the rockets. Come on, Chips.'

The two men bounded to their transporter and a moment or two later were speeding towards the launch site.

'Do you know how to decommission these things?' Chips said.

'Don't have to.' Raven shook his head. 'We can do that later. All we have to do is deactivate the countdown sequence initiators. Then we can denuke them at our leisure. Not the sort of thing you want to do quickly.'

'The control room.' Chips pointed to his left. 'It's over there.'

As quickly as they could, they made it into the room. There, slumped in the corner snoring softly, were two men Raven immediately recognized as Hassad and Aziz from pictures he had been shown.

'Just as well they took their helmets off,' said Raven. 'If they hadn't they'd have had their own oxygen supply. He looked around him. 'What's beyond that door?' he asked.

'A corridor that leads to the crew room.'

'Crew room?'

Chips nodded. 'Just before a manned flight takes off, the crew pass through here for a final briefing. Then they go to the crew room and from there up in an elevator that runs up the outside of their rocket.' He pointed at the rockets outside. 'You can see the elevators there.'

'Where are the countdown sequence initiators?'

'Over there.' Chips nodded to a line of red buttons on a control panel. 'By the window.'

Raven looked at the buttons. 'Blast!' he said through gritted teeth. '*Three* of them are activated.'

'Looks like you'll have to deal with all three.'

'Thanks, buddy!'

Chips watched intently as Raven very gently turned the first of the buttons to the right and began to unscrew the cap. The wires underneath looked like strands of red, yellow and green wool knitted into a multi-coloured ball.

'Hope you know what you're doing,' Chips sighed as Raven cut through first one then another and another of the wires with a pair of laser cutters.

''Course I do,' said Raven, hoping he sounded more confident than he felt.

'One down, two to go,' he said a minute or two later and started to unscrew the second cap.

Both men were so involved in what Raven was doing they didn't hear the faint moan from behind. They didn't hear the sound of someone stirring. They didn't hear someone tiptoeing across the floor, and slipping through the door Raven had asked about earlier. And until it was too late, they didn't hear someone else pad towards them.

Raven had just finished defusing the second button when Chips gasped aloud and slumped to the floor. Raven spun round just in time to see Aziz standing behind them, a vicious-looking spanner in his hand.

Quick as a flash he dodged to one side.

A split second later Aziz brought the spanner flashing downwards.

It shattered a glass panel, sending a shower of shards flying in all directions.

Raven lifted his right leg, spun round like a dancer, and brought his foot into the back of Aziz's legs.

There was a pained cry as the terrorist's legs buckled under him and another when Raven threw himself on top of him.

The two men rolled over and over, fists flying, legs kicking.

For a moment it looked as though Aziz was winning. He sat on Raven's chest raining blows down on him.

But Raven was the more powerful of the two. With one arch of his back, he sent Aziz shooting backwards through the air, clambered to his knees and dived towards him. Aziz grunted as Raven's head slammed into his chest, knocking the air from his lungs.

'OK. Where's Hassad?' Raven gripped Aziz by the collar and dragged him to his feet.

The only answer he got was to be spat at.

Raven's hands tightened around Aziz's throat. 'I said where's Hassad?'

But before Aziz could answer there was a loud roar and the room shook like a roller coaster.

'What the – ' gasped Raven, spinning round to see Chips sprawled on the ignition-control panel. As Raven leapt across the room to pull him off it, through the window he could see rocket exhaust billowing around outside.

And then, out of the orange cloud, the snub-nosed rocket in Bay 5 rose slowly in the air, hovered there for a second then shot heavenward.

'No!' wailed Aziz, dropping to his knees.

'What's the matter?' shouted Raven. 'Scared of a little noise?'

'Hassad!' screamed Aziz, pointing to the flash of light streaking through the sky. 'He was hiding in that rocket!'

* * * * *

'It was pure luck, sir,' said Raven, putting his cup down on a coaster on the President's desk. 'The two switches I deactivated were the ones that would have fired the nukes. The third one launched the rocket Hassad was hiding in.'

'And this Chips person fired it accidentally?'

'Yes, sir,' Raven nodded. 'He came to when I was

fighting Aziz and tried to stand up. Unfortunately his legs gave way and he fell on top of the launch control panel, initiating the final countdown sequence.'

'You mean you had no idea which two of the three live buttons fired the nukes' engines?' said Mrs Gates, who was sitting beside her husband.

'Right, ma'am.'

'So when this security person slumped on the panel there was a three to one chance he might have fired one of the nuclear warheads?'

'Yes, ma'am!'

The President and his wife shuddered.

'How come they woke up?' asked Mrs Gates. 'Aziz and Hassad?'

'The oxygen supply to the launch site was faulty.'

'And where is Hassad now?'

'Shooting for the stars, sir.'

'Well, son.' The President put his cup on the table, got to his feet and held out his hand. 'All I can say is that your country thanks you. Now if you'll excuse me I'd better call the Chinese Emperor.'

Raven shook the President's hand, nodded politely to Mrs Gates and left the room.

As the guard closed the door behind him, he heard the First Lady's voice raised in anger. 'Listen, you Tennessee tramp, how many times do I have to tell you to use a coaster!'

THE DARK SIDE

For centuries, people called the side of the Moon that we never see from Earth 'The Dark Side'. But it is not dark there. Days there are just as bright as they are on other parts of the Moon. And today, scientists call the Dark Side 'The Far Side'.

THE MOON – NO MAN'S LAND

The United States' National Aeronautics and Space Administration, NASA, is leading the way in planning how to set up bases, research stations and manned colonies on the Moon. But the US and most other countries believe that the cost is too great for any one country to afford on its own.

They believe that space is territory that cannot be claimed by any one nation. On the Moon the boundaries that exist between countries on Earth will no longer matter. Major breakthroughs in science and technology will become possible as great minds from many countries combine to solve the problems involved in allowing men and women to live for any length of time on the Moon.

MEN ON THE MOON

Since 1986, NASA has been working on plans to establish the first permanent base on the surface of the Moon. Their plans are now so far advanced they are already looking at likely sites.

One idea they are considering is to land a small, inflatable module which will accommodate a crew of four for around two weeks.

As time passes, more of these modules will be landed. Initially they will be as small as the first one. But as space flight becomes more and more accessible, larger modules will be established on the lunar surface.

SEEING STARS

Once a permanent lunar base has been established, one of the first tasks astronauts will face will be to build radio telescopes on the Far Side of the Moon. Because there is little or no radio interference there, astronomers will be able to probe much deeper into space than they can on Earth. The lack of artificial light on the Moon will also give astronomers there startlingly clear images of the stars and planets.

Take-Off From Mars

If human beings ever reach Mars, it is more than likely that they will blast off from a base on the Moon. Many of the parts needed to build such a base would be manufactured on the International Space Station or one of the other space stations in low-Earth orbit and taken to the Moon when needed. Other, larger, parts would be made on the Moon.

Why launch from the Moon? Because a spacecraft launched from the Moon doesn't need to carry the fuel required to overcome the Earth's gravity and air resistance.

Many years ago, people scoffed at an author who called the Moon 'Mankind's gateway to the Universe'. If NASA predictions come true, it is he who will have the last laugh.

Fill 'Er Up Please

Within the next hundred years, fuel stations will be established on the Moon. Astronauts travelling through cislunar space – the region of outer space between the Earth and the Moon – will be able to land on the Moon and refuel their spacecraft. This means that when they take off from Earth they will not have to carry fuel for the return journey.

THE X-30

Late-twentieth-century spacecraft are multi-stage machines. But since 1986, NASA scientists and experts from the US Air Force have been developing the technology they hope to use to put a single-stage spacecraft, the X-30, into space.

The X-30 will be about 55 metres (180 feet) long and weigh around 150 tonnes. It will be built from heat-resistant metals such as titanium.

The engines being developed for the X-30 are known as supersonic ramjets or scramjets, powerful enough to take the spaceship to about 28,000 km/h (17,500 mph) – the speed that the craft needs to reach in order to beat the Earth's gravity and go into orbit.

The extra power needed to achieve full 'orbital velocity' will be provided by rocket engines fuelled by liquid oxygen and liquid hydrogen carried in tanks at the back of the fuselage.

Once in space, rocket engines will power the craft to its destination. The fuel tanks for these will probably take up most of the top part of the spaceplane.